Blind Trust

Shay Jackson

Bein' Good

Blind Trust

Fitting In

Holding Back

Keepin' Her Man

ISBN-13: 978-1-61651-776-2
ISBN-10: 1-61651-776-X
eBook: 978-1-61247-338-3

Printed in Guangzhou, China
0112/CA21200064

16 15 14 13 12   1 2 3 4 5

[chapter]

1

Sherise stared down at her textbook. She felt that old, familiar feeling. The feeling you get when you have no idea how to even begin to solve a math problem. If she couldn't solve the first one, how would she solve the other nineteen that were due tomorrow?

So there she sat. Pencil in hand. Scratch paper in front of her. Math book open. But the problems on the page all blurred together into one big mess of numbers, letters, and weird symbols. Sherise hated algebra. *Hated* it. What the hell did letters have to do with math anyway?

Sherise looked across the library table at Tia. Tia didn't seem to have any issues with the problems. She sat there, furiously scribbling with her pencil and solving the problems with ease.

It didn't help matters that Marnyke was in the room, flapping her jaws. Marnyke had the biggest mouth of any girl in school. She talked nonstop. And she usually was talking about herself. Marnyke didn't seem to care that she was sitting in the middle of the library during study hall. She yelled out her story like she was telling it to someone standing right next to a speaker at a concert.

"That's when I knew," Marnyke hollered, "*knew* I had to have him. Any man that can handle himself on the street *and* on the court, he's all mine. For real."

Sherise slammed her pencil down dramatically. Why did Marnyke have to be such a big-mouth all the time? Why was she always yelling and being so annoying? Tia noticed that Sherise was frustrated.

"Doing okay on those problems?" Tia asked Sherise.

Sherise exhaled. "It's just hard to focus in here."

Tia nodded. "You got that right," she said, glaring over at Marnyke. "Who is she talking about anyway?"

Sherise looked over her shoulder to see if Marnyke was listening. Then she whispered, "I think she's talking about Darnell."

Sherise liked Darnell. He lived in the same high-rise apartment complex she did. Sometimes Sherise was jealous of Marnyke. She got to run wild, do whatever she wanted. That's why she got to hang with Darnell. Darnell got to do whatever he wanted too. Sherise, on the other hand, was on lockdown. Her stepdad kept her on a tight leash. She never got to do anything cool.

Sherise sighed and looked back at her book. "Did we even go over these kinds of problems in class, Tia? I don't remember a thing that looked like these. I mean, I get number one. But what about number two? It's like a foreign language!"

Tia moved her chair closer to Sherise's to help her. But as she did, the bell rang. The school day was over. "I can help you with these tomorrow if you want," Tia said. "Or, I bet your sister knows how to do them."

"Oh, I'm sure she does," Sherise said sarcastically, packing up her things. "No way I'm askin' her for help."

Tia gave Sherise a kind look. "You coming to YC tomorrow?" Tia asked. "Or do you have to work?"

"I'll be there," Sherise said, pulling out a compact from her purse. She checked her makeup quickly in the small mirror. Then she closed the compact. She wasn't very good with numbers. But she was damn good when it came to maintaining her look.

"I work tonight, though," Sherise said. "I gotta roll to catch my bus. I'll holler at you later, Tia."

"*Hasta luego*," Tia said. "See you later."

Sherise walked quickly to a bus stop near the school. She was tired and frustrated. It wasn't so much the algebra. It was her boring life. The last thing she felt like doing was unloading boxes at GG's Clothing. But that's exactly what she was on her way to do. That was her life.

On the bus ride to the Southside Mall, Sherise dug her name tag out of her purse. *Sherise Butler, Receiving Associate*. Then it had the GG's Clothing logo at the bottom. The job wasn't all that great. Just opening boxes and stocking shelves and clothing racks. But at least her boss, Juanita, was cool. And it was great having her own money. More importantly, the employee discount was great for her wardrobe.

Sherise hopped off the bus at the mall and hustled into GG's. As usual, she punched in her timecard and grabbed a box cutter. She felt pretty sorry for herself. What would her life be like if she could do whatever she wanted? Would she hang out in rough crowds? Go to wild parties and date bad boys?

"Hey, girl," Juanita said, looking at her watch. "Cutting it a little close aren't ya? What, you think I won't fire you?"

Sherise smiled. "What up, Juanita. Where do you want me to start today?"

Juanita led Sherise to a corner of the receiving room. "Why don't you start with these," Juanita said. "They're the most exciting things we got in right now.

First shipment too. Open one up. Let's see what's in there."

Sherise opened the box cutter and cut the tape on one of the boxes. It had a different logo on the outside. "Never seen this brand before," Sherise said, opening up the cardboard folds. Inside was a new line of handbags. Sherise grabbed the top one and held it up. It had an amazing purple and blue houndstooth pattern.

"How much you think these will go for?" Sherise said, eyeing the bag carefully. "You know, retail?"

Juanita stared longingly at the bag too. "Two hundred at least," Juanita estimated.

Sherise put the bag's strap over her shoulder. It was a great bag. "This bag is *hot*," Sherise said. "I *love* it!"

Juanita grabbed her clipboard. Then she put her pen behind her ear. "You think you're getting a raise or something? Maybe a fairy godmother sometime soon? If not, you best forget about that bag," Juanita joked.

Sherise smiled and set the handbag down. She finished unpacking five more boxes of them. The handbags really were amazing. Sherise decided she would save up her money and buy one for sure. She wanted to be the first girl at school to carry one. Sherise finished her three-hour shift. She said good-bye to Juanita and hurried to the bus. Sherise wanted to make it home in time for dinner.

She barely made the bus! Sherise had to practically run out in front of the bus to get it to stop. It was better than being late for dinner though. That was probably worse than getting hit by a bus.

On the bus, Sherise found an empty seat and sat down. She gave a loud sigh. What a day. All she wanted to do was go home and lay on the couch. She put on her headphones and started playing her favorite song. Sherise closed her eyes and listened to it carefully.

Sherise always studied the songs she performed. She was going to sing it in front of a crowd this Friday night! She had to know every nuance, every key change perfectly.

She cranked the volume and moved her head with the rhythm. She was in her own world, getting inside her song. But in the second verse, Sherise got a funny feeling someone was watching her.

"That Robert Johnson?" a voice asked. "I thought no one listened to that old stuff no more."

Sherise opened her eyes. It was Carlos. He was standing right in front of her. He was holding onto the overhead rail.

Sherise could feel her heart racing as she took off her headphones.

"It's my song," she blurted out. "I mean, I'm singing it. This Friday. At the Northeast Meet-Up."

Carlos nodded. "I've been to one of those," Carlos said. "Your dad, he runs those things, right?"

"He's my stepdad," Sherise replied. "My real dad was a musician. He ... he died."

Carlos took one hand off the overhead handrail. He adjusted his backpack. Sherise instantly felt stupid. Why had she just told him that her dad died? What the hell was wrong with her? That's when she noticed that she still had her name tag on too. What a great impression she was making.

"This is my stop," Carlos said. He ducked down to see out the bus window. He was so tall! Sherise nodded and looked down shyly. She wished she could just disappear. She was so embarrassed.

Carlos walked to the rear exit. He stepped down one step then turned back to her. "Maybe I'll come hear what you got this Friday," he said. Then he pushed the doors open and hopped off the bus.

Sherise was thrilled. Maybe she hadn't blown it! She had on a pretty cute outfit that day. Except for her damn name tag. She dug out her compact and checked her makeup. Not too bad for the end of the day! She couldn't believe that Carlos had talked to her. She'd had a crush on him all year. But he kind of blew hot and cold. It was hard to tell how much he was into her.

When Sherise got to her building, she tried to tone the smiling down a bit. Sherise didn't want her family to ask her any questions. When she walked into her apartment, her twin sister, Kiki, greeted her coldly.

"Thanks for hurrying home," Kiki

said, setting a bowl of mashed potatoes on the table. "I'm gonna be late to the game 'cause of you."

"Whatever, Kiki," Sherise snapped. "Do you know what I had to do to catch the bus? I practically got run over!"

Tyson, the twins' stepdad, told the girls to stop bickering. He said to sit down. Their mother, LaTreece, joined them. She was wiping her hands on a towel as she came from the kitchen. They all sat down. Tyson said grace. When he finished, they all started eating.

Kiki ate quickly. Her plate was clean in under a minute. "Mom, Tyson, the game starts in forty minutes," Kiki said, wiping off her mouth. "May I be excused?"

Suddenly, Sherise remembered that Carlos was on the basketball team. "Me too?" she blurted out, setting her fork down quickly. Sherise had never shown interest in going to games before. Everyone was a little shocked. But LaTreece and Tyson agreed that both girls could go.

"Just hurry up, all right?" Kiki shrugged into her girls' basketball team hoodie. "No takin' four hours to put on your face. I'm not missin' tip-off."

Sherise changed her clothes fast. She grabbed her makeup bag. Sherise could touch it up on the bus. She was really excited to see Carlos play ball! The girls ran out of their building to the bus stop.

[chapter]

2

When Sherise and Kiki arrived at the school, they headed to the gym. The bleachers were packed!

"Looks like we made it just in time," Kiki said, standing in the doorway of the gymnasium. The South Central Tigers were still warming up.

Sherise peeked into the gym. She spotted Carlos on the court right away. She watched him receive a pass from Darnell. Then he moved toward the basket, slowly at first, then moving faster as he approached the hoop. Sherise couldn't believe how good he looked doing a layup! He was so fine in his uniform! Sherise tried her best not to stare at him. But she had a hard time looking away.

Kiki scanned the bleachers. "There's Marnyke and Nishell," she said. "Wanna sit with them?"

Sherise's stomach dropped. Marnyke was the last person she wanted to sit by. "Let's sit there, right by the court," Sherise said, pointing to an open spot in the second row around mid-court. Kiki agreed.

As Sherise and Kiki walked to the seats, Sherise wondered if Carlos would notice her. Had he seen her in the doorway? Did he see her now, as she walked along the edge of the court? Sherise was too nervous to look his way. Instead, she stared straight ahead and sat down.

Once seated, Sherise's eyes moved right back to Carlos on the court. He was standing in a semicircle with his teammates. They were all gathered around the coach, who was busy scribbling on a whiteboard.

The announcer was introducing the visiting team's players. Hardly anyone was paying attention.

Suddenly there was a burst of music and the announcer got much louder. "And now ... the starting lineup for your South Central Tigers!" the voice boomed over the sound system.

Everyone in the stands stood up and clapped as each player's position, number, and name was announced. Sherise tried to control herself. She didn't want to overdo it! Still, her heart beat so fast as she watched Carlos run out onto the court when his name was called.

Then it was time for the game to begin. The starters took to the court. Sherise watched nervously as a referee tossed the basketball up in the air at center court.

Darnell got the ball off the tip-off. He passed it to Carlos. Carlos moved quickly toward the right side of the court. A defender was close at his side. Carlos took two huge steps just before the basket. He leaped up into the air. So did the defender. At the last moment, Carlos passed the ball to Darnell. Darnell jammed the ball in the basket.

Sherise rose to her feet and screamed. “Way to go, Carlos and Darnell!” she yelled, clapping and smiling. Then she turned back to Kiki, who was sitting down and clapping.

“Kiki!” Sherise yelled. “Did you see that? Did you see how Carlos fooled the defender like that? And then Darnell finished it. Bam!”

Kiki looked at her oddly. Sherise was clumsily imitating Carlos’s move.

"Oh, I saw it," Kiki replied. "I also see why you wanted to come to the game."

Sherise did her best to play dumb. "What's that supposed to mean?"

Kiki arched her eyebrows. She stared back at Sherise. "You've got a thing for Carlos, don't you?" Kiki asked.

Sherise sat back down on the bleachers. "Get real, Kiki. I hardly even know him," Sherise said.

"Oh, so I'm supposed to believe that you're here 'cause you all of a sudden care 'bout b-ball?"

Sherise was about to snap back at her sister. But she held it in. Marnyke and Nishell were coming toward them.

"What up, sluts!" Marnyke yelled. She and Nishell were squeezing themselves in behind the twins on the bleachers.

"Hey, Mar. What up, Shell," Kiki said.

Sherise gave Marnyke and Nishell a cool smile. Then she turned back to the game just in time to see Darnell nail a three-pointer from the baseline.

"Looks like it's gonna be another blowout. My man Darnell's got this game, no prob," Marnyke said.

"Yeah, with him and Carlos on the team, we've got a good shot at going to State this year," Kiki replied.

Marnyke lowered her head down between Sherise and Kiki. Kiki made a funny face. "Damn, Mar," Kiki said. "You smell like a barroom. You best be careful. There are teachers all over the place."

Marnyke laughed. "You Butler girls. Always worried 'bout every little thing. That's 'bout the only thing you got in common! We got one little gym rat here," Marnyke joked, pulling Kiki's hoodie up over her head. "And one *princess*," she finished, looking over at Sherise.

Sherise hated it when Marnyke did that. She was always trying to drive

Sherise and Kiki apart. Kiki didn't see it that way. Marnyke didn't bother her. In fact, Kiki thought Marnyke was kind of funny.

Kiki pulled her hoodie back down. She smiled back at Marnyke. "Someone's gotta worry 'bout you, Marnyke," Kiki said. "It's pretty much a full-time job."

"Don't you be worryin' 'bout me," Marnyke said. "I'm straight. Me and my girl Nishell here. We are on our way to a party. You girls in? This game will last a couple hours. Your stepdad won't know you left, as long as you go home at the right time."

Kiki shook her head. "Nah, I wanna see the game," she said. Sherise nodded.

"Suit yourselves, Butler saints," Marnyke teased. "Let's roll, Shell."

Nishell said good-bye to the twins. Then she followed Marnyke out of the gym. Sherise was happy to see them go.

"That girl drives me *crazy*," Sherise said.

Kiki kept her eyes on the court but shook her head. "I don't know why you let her get to you," Kiki said.

Sherise rolled her eyes and looked back out at the court. Carlos was trying to bring the ball up the court. But a defender was all over him like a shadow. The defender batted the ball away from Carlos's control and scored!

Sherise asked Kiki, "What the hell? How did that just happen?"

"It happens," Kiki said. "Plus, Carlos seems a little off tonight."

Sherise didn't like the sound of that. "Why?" she asked Kiki.

"What, do I look like a sports doctor or something? He's just havin' an off night, that's all. It happens."

Despite the fact that Carlos didn't have his best game, South Central High still won, but only by five points. When the final buzzer rang, everyone got up to leave. Sherise grabbed Kiki's arm. "Maybe we should talk to him," Sherise suggested.

Kiki looked at her like she was nuts. "Talk to Carlos? About what?"

"You know, why he was off tonight."

Kiki rolled her eyes. "You got it bad, Reesie. For real. I never seen you so twisted."

"Please, Kiki?" Sherise begged.

"All right. But you're doin' all the talkin'," Kiki said.

The girls hung out in the stands while everyone else filed out of the gym. Soon Carlos came out of the locker room with Darnell. Sherise said, "There he is, Kiki. Come on."

As they walked toward the guys, Sherise got butterflies in her stomach. "You know him from basketball camp and stuff, Kiki. Just ask him some question about the game."

"Say what?" Kiki yelled. "I said *you* had to do the talkin'!"

Sherise pulled Kiki along. Halfheartedly, Kiki walked with Sherise to the other side of the gym. Carlos was talking to Darnell about the game. The closer she and Kiki got to him, the more Sherise's heart raced.

"What up, Carlos, Darnell," Kiki said, holding out her hand.

Both boys slapped Kiki's hand. "Hey, girls, what up," Darnell said.

Carlos looked at Sherise. He gave her a small nod.

"Nice breakaway in the second half, Carlos," Kiki said.

"Thanks. But it wasn't my best night out there," he replied sadly.

Sherise couldn't help herself. "Why?" she blurted out. "What's wrong?"

Carlos looked at her with disgust in his eyes. "What? You got a way out for me? Maybe at your little Meet-Up?" he said meanly. "Think you know how to fix everything?"

Sherise clenched her fists and raised her chin. She was so insulted. She had just been trying to help. "Come on, Kiki," she said, glaring at Carlos. "Let's go."

Kiki froze for a moment. She gave Carlos an *I'm sorry* look. Kiki shrugged her shoulders as if to say, "I don't know what's with her." She then followed Sherise toward the exit.

Carlos and Darnell watched them head for the door. Darnell said, "Hey, man, don't take your bad game out on Sherise. She's a sweet girl."

Carlos got in Darnell's face. "How you know she's sweet? You hot for her?"

Darnell raised his hands. "Chill out, bro," he said. "We're just friends. Marnyke is more than enough for me to handle. But if you want Sherise, I wouldn't go pissin' her off like that."

Carlos looked toward the twins. They were about to leave the almost empty gym. "Gotta go," he said. "Later, bro." He gave Darnell a fist bump.

Darnell smirked as Carlos grabbed his gym bag and ran after Kiki and Sherise. "That boy's got it bad," he thought.

"Wait up," Carlos called out. Sherise turned toward him. Her eyes were beginning to tear up. But she promised herself she would not cry.

"Look, I'm sorry. I didn't mean to snap on y'all. I just ... I got some things on my mind."

Sherise backed off. "I wish I could help in some way, that's all," she said, as if nothing had happened.

Carlos was confused by Sherise's concern. He looked to Kiki for an explanation. But Kiki couldn't give one. Carlos exhaled loudly. Then he began talking.

"It's my ma," he said. He explained that the bank was going to take his mom's car away. She hadn't made any payments in some months now.

"I know a guy who can give me the money tomorrow," Carlos said. "But he lives outside of the city. I got no way to get there. Buses don't run out that far."

Sherise listened to Carlos's story. "I can give you a ride," she volunteered. "I could use my stepdad's car."

Again, Carlos looked to Kiki. "Is she for real?" he asked.

Kiki raised her eyebrows. "She's for real, all right."

To Kiki's surprise, Sherise and Carlos made something of a plan. Sherise would borrow her stepdad's car. She and Carlos would skip seventh period together tomorrow. They would go get the money. Then Sherise could make it back in time for family dinner.

Once the plan was set, Sherise, Kiki, and Carlos walked out of the gym into the night. They stood for a moment outside the school. The parking lot was almost empty. “We gotta catch our bus,” Kiki said. “Let’s go, Sherise. Peace out, Carlos.”

“Later, Kiki,” Carlos said. Then he locked eyes with Sherise. He didn’t know what to say. He looked down at the ground, then back at Sherise.

“It’s really no big deal, Carlos,” Sherise said. “Really. See ya tomorrow.”

Carlos nodded and looked back out at the parking lot. “Okay. See you tomorrow,” he said.

Sherise didn’t want to turn away. She could have stood there all night with Carlos! But instead, she went to join Kiki at their bus stop. Carlos headed the other way to catch his bus.

[chapter]

3

As they waited at the bus stop, Kiki said, "What the hell is wrong with you? You think Tyson is going to let you take his car? So you can drive Carlos to some crack shack? It's probably some guy that owes Carlos money for drugs," Kiki said.

Sherise knew her sister was right. And it scared her. She had no idea who owed Carlos this money or why. All she knew was that just standing next to Carlos set her whole body on fire. And if Carlos needed a ride somewhere, she wanted to give it to him.

"Relax, Kiki," Sherise said. "I'm sure it's totally legit."

"Oh yeah?" Kiki said. "You sure 'bout that? I'm not."

"Come on, Kiki," Sherise started. "All you have to do is cover for me at yearbook club tomorrow. Just say I'm workin', they'll believe that."

The bus arrived and both girls got on and walked to the back.

Just before the bus pulled away, Darnell ran up and got on too. He sat next to Sherise. "Looks like our little Reesie's got a boyfriend," Darnell teased in a singsong voice.

Kiki snorted. "Yeah, and she's bein' a fool for him already. She's gonna skip seventh period tomorrow so she can drive him who knows where to get some cash from who knows who. Probably some crackhead drug dealer. I know he's done some dealin' himself."

"Not no more," Darnell said. "Yeah, he used to be in that life. Me too. But we got out. Went straight. He does a little weed now and then, but he's not dealin'."

"See, Kiki?" Sherise said smugly. "I knew it."

"You're still a fool if you skip school and go drivin' him all over town in Tyson's car," Kiki said.

Sherise did not respond. She spent the rest of the bus ride looking out the window. She didn't want to discuss this anymore with her sister.

They all got off at the Northeast Towers stop. Kiki and Sherise said good-bye to Darnell and went to their building.

In the elevator, Kiki's phone buzzed. It was a text from Marnyke. "Hey girl. What u up 2? U missin a good time. c u 2morro."

Once inside the apartment, Sherise saw the light was on in her parents' bedroom. She took a deep breath and knocked on the door.

"Come in," her mom said.

Sherise opened the door. "Hi, Momma. Hey, Tyson," Sherise said sweetly.

"How was the game, baby?" LaTreece asked.

"Good. We won."

Sherise lingered in the doorway until her mom said, "What's on your mind, baby?"

"Well, I wanted to ask if I could use your car tomorrow, Tyson."

"Can't you take the bus?" Tyson said.

"There's this outfit I want at the Eastside Mall," Sherise said. "If I have the car, I can hit the mall before the yearbook club meeting. Please, Tyson? The outfit is for this Friday, you know, for the Meet-Up."

Tyson agreed to let Sherise take his car. "I'll take the bus to work tomorrow," Tyson said. "It's good for me to check in on public transportation in this city once in a while."

Sherise smiled. "Thank you, Tyson!"

Sherise hurried to the bedroom she shared with Kiki. She pulled a notebook and a pen out of her bag. She tried to write a believable note to excuse her from seventh period tomorrow.

Kiki looked over at what she was doing. "You're insane, you know that?" Kiki said. But Sherise didn't care. She kept working on her forged note. Her fourteenth draft was a keeper. Then Sherise fell asleep. She dreamt about what it would be like to spend a whole afternoon alone with Carlos.

The next morning, Sherise woke up extra early. She wanted to look good for her day with Carlos! She put on her newest jeans and a pink tank top. Then she moved all of her things out of her black handbag and into her pink one. Sherise walked out into the kitchen like a woman about to rob a bank. Her mom was making coffee. Tyson was reading the paper. Kiki was eating cereal.

"Good morning, baby," her mom said.

Tyson folded up his paper. "Girls, glad you're both here. Your mom and I have something to tell you," Tyson said. Sherise and Kiki looked across the table at each other. It sounded like Tyson was about to announce that they were going to have a new little sister or brother or something!

But that wasn't the case. Instead, Tyson told the twins that he had accepted a new position as a community redevelopment leader. "This position," he began, "it's a step up. A big step up."

"All right!" Kiki joked. "So we're gonna be rich now, right?"

Tyson shook his head and smiled. "Not exactly. This new job comes with more political clout. But less money than my old job."

Sherise looked over to her mother. Money was already tight in their family. Now things were going to get tighter? It was hard to imagine.

"This job has its setbacks," Tyson said. "But it gives me room to do more. More programs. More resources. I'll be able to make a real difference in the community."

No one in the family spoke much after Tyson's announcement. Everyone was thinking the same thing. *Less money.* Kiki finished her cereal. Then she broke the silence. "Come on, Sherise. We best roll."

Sherise nodded, then looked to Tyson. "Tyson, can I have the car keys?" she asked in a soft voice.

"Oh, right. The keys," Tyson said, smiling and handing the keys to Sherise. "See you girls at dinner," he said.

Sherise and Kiki ran down the stairs. They walked to Tyson's car, which was parked on the street outside their building. Sherise got behind the wheel. The girls headed to school. Sherise parked in the back of the overflow lot at their school.

"Tell me you're not really gonna try to use that whack note you wrote last night," Kiki said. Kiki closed the car door. Sherise shot her a glaring look.

"It will work," Sherise said.

Kiki rolled her eyes. "Good luck with that," she said. They entered the main doors of the school. Kiki stopped in the bathroom, and Sherise continued toward her locker.

As Sherise walked up to her locker, she saw Carlos waiting there for her. Her heart rose up in her throat. She tried to keep her cool. But she had a hell of time doing that when it came to Carlos.

"What up," Carlos said uneasily. His hands were in his pockets.

"Hey," Sherise replied, smiling.

"So, Sherise. I been thinkin'. I appreciate your offer and all," Carlos started, "but I don't wanna get you into my family mess. It just ain't right."

The smile left Sherise's face. "Carlos, it's no big deal. For *real*. I just need to be home by seven for dinner. That's all."

Carlos rubbed his hand across his forehead. "You got the car?" he asked.

Sherise nodded.

"Show me."

Sherise and Carlos stepped outside the main doors. Sherise pointed out her stepdad's car. "It's in the second lot. See that little red one? In the row farthest from us?"

Carlos took a deep breath. "All right. Meet ya there. Few minutes after sixth period is over. You cool?"

"Yep."

The bell rang. Sherise and Carlos parted ways.

The rest of the school day seemed to drag on for Sherise. Especially algebra. She never did finish her homework. The teacher covered new material too. Sherise was slipping even farther behind. But she couldn't think about algebra now. She had bigger things to worry about.

Sherise watched the clock as the last minutes of sixth period passed. The bell rang. She headed to the office with her fake note. The woman behind the desk looked at the note. All of a sudden, Sherise felt nervous. Then the woman looked at Sherise.

"Good luck at your doctor's appointment, hon," the woman said.

All right! Sherise couldn't believe it! The note worked! She walked quickly to her locker and grabbed her things.

“Where you think you’re goin’?” Nishell asked as Sherise closed her locker.

Sherise was startled. She had thought she was alone in the hallway. But there Nishell stood. She was staring at Sherise.

“Doctor. Gotta run,” Sherise replied. She would not look Nishell in the eye.

“Lucky,” Nishell said, looking around the hall. “That’s better than English. I’ve got a hangover like you wouldn’t believe. That party last night was off the hook.”

Sherise smiled nervously. “Oh, that’s cool,” she said. “Yeah, Kiki got a text from Marnyke. Mar said it was the bomb.”

Nishell nodded. “So you comin’ to YC after your appointment?” Nishell asked.

“No, I gotta work,” Sherise said. She was starting to sweat. Sherise wasn’t a very good liar. Then her phone buzzed. Sherise ignored it.

“You’re not lookin’ to see who’s after you, girl?” Now Nishell was onto Sherise.

"Probably just my doctor's office confirmin' my appointment. Really. I gotta split." Sherise was down the hall before Nishell could say another word.

Nishell nodded. "Word. Well, I gotta get to class," she said to herself with a smirk. "See you tomorrow."

Sherise hurried out of the school and across the parking lot. She dug the car keys out of her purse. Sherise felt a rush throughout her body. She couldn't believe she was actually skipping school! Sherise had never skipped before in her whole life.

Carlos was busy going about skipping class too. Like Nishell, he had English last period. Carlos told the teacher he had to use the bathroom. But instead of going to the bathroom, he slipped into the gym. He walked through the guys' locker room, then into an equipment room. Carlos made his way carefully and quietly through the portable basketball hoops and chairs that were stored there. He made it to the back of the room. Carlos felt around for the handle to the emergency door.

He found it! Then he turned the handle and was out the door. Carlos knew the alarm on the door didn't work. He had used this escape route many times before. Carlos adjusted his eyes as he stepped out into the afternoon sunlight. He ran to Sherise's car.

Sherise was slouched down in the driver's seat. Then she saw Carlos coming. Instantly her heart rate climbed. She looked in the rear view mirror. Her makeup was okay. Her hair was looking pretty good too—straight and smooth. Sherise tugged at her tank top a bit. She adjusted her bra. Sherise then tossed her handbag into the back seat. Carlos opened the passenger door.

"Hey," he said with a smile. "You ready to roll?"

"Yeah, where we goin'?" Sherise asked.

Carlos got in the car. He looked around nervously. "Get on the freeway," he said. "Take Broadway over to ..."

Sherise smiled. She interrupted him. "Broadway to Forty-fifth Street. I *know* how to get on the freeway, Carlos."

Carlos smiled back at her. "Thatta girl," he said. He looked over his shoulder. Then he slouched low, hoping no one would see him. He exhaled loudly.

As Sherise pulled out of the parking lot, they heard the tardy bell ring in the school. Seventh period was starting. The hallways were empty except for a few students. Including Nishell.

Nishell had a sneaky feeling about her run-in with Sherise. She stopped at the main doors of the school. She looked out into the parking lot.

Nishell saw Sherise's car pull out of the lot. But Sherise wasn't alone on her way to her so-called doctor's appointment. Nishell clearly saw two heads in the car. She got to English class late. Surprise! Carlos was nowhere in sight. "Wait till everyone hears about this!" she thought. She pulled out her phone and started texting.

Meanwhile, Sherise took Broadway to Forty-fifth Street. She felt great once they were on the freeway. Everything had worked out! She couldn't help but feel excited inside. Sherise looked over at Carlos. She smiled. And then giggled.

"What?" Carlos asked, smiling back at her.

"I can't believe we're doin' this!" Sherise squealed.

"What, you never cut class before?" Carlos asked.

Sherise kept her eyes on the road. She kept smiling. "Nope," she replied happily.

Carlos smiled and looked out the passenger window. "Damn, girl. You makin' me feel like it's *my* first time again," Carlos said. "You and me. We gotta do this more often."

Sherise looked over at Carlos. She felt happier and more alive than she could ever remember feeling.

[chapter]

4

Sherise and Carlos drove south on the freeway. There was an obvious energy between them.

"You surprised me last night," Carlos said.

"What do you mean?" Sherise asked.

"Your sister Kiki comes to all the home games. You never been there before. Why?"

Sherise shrugged. "I work a lot," she replied. "And I'm not *that* into basketball. No offense."

"So why did you come out last night?" Carlos pressed.

Sherise tightened her hands on the wheel. "You know how we ran into each other on the bus yesterday? Well, you said you were gonna come hear me sing at the Meet-Up. So, I wanted to come see you play ball."

Carlos laughed out loud. "I feel you," he said. "You had to see for yourself. I see how it is."

"Somethin' like that," Sherise said with a smile. That Carlos noticed her made her feel special. And he knew how often she came to basketball games.

"Fair is fair, Sherise," Carlos said seriously. "You saw me play ball last night. Now I get to hear you sing. Let's hear it. Robert Johnson. Right here. Right now."

"In the car?" Sherise exclaimed.

"Uh-huh."

"Not gonna happen," Sherise replied. "I said I'd *drive* you. I didn't say I'd entertain you too."

Carlos laughed again.

"Besides," Sherise continued. "Singin' the blues isn't like that. You can't just belt it out. Ya have to feel it. Have to be in the mood."

"You just playin' me now," Carlos teased.

"No, for real. You have to, like, I don't know. Be a little sad or down. To sing it right. You feel me?"

"And you're not sad right now, yeah?" Carlos asked.

"I'm feelin' no pain right now," Sherise smiled.

Carlos's phone buzzed. He didn't even look to see who it was. Sherise was feeling like nothing else mattered. It was just her and Carlos.

Sherise and Carlos both sat in silence for a few minutes as they raced down the freeway. But then their chatter returned. They were surprised how easy it was for them to talk to each other. They were both into what each other had to say. The miles flew by.

"Whoa, hold up. This is the exit," Carlos said pointing to an upcoming off-ramp. Sherise hit her blinker and made a quick exit. Carlos directed Sherise to a house in a rundown neighborhood not far off of the freeway. Suddenly, the good vibe in the car changed to tension.

"Here, stop here," Carlos ordered. Sherise parked and looked at Carlos. She couldn't help it. She was scared.

"Stay in the car, all right?" Carlos said. He sensed fear in her eyes. "And lock the doors too. I won't be long."

Carlos opened the car door and got out. Before he closed it, he looked in at Sherise. "Thanks for doing this," he said quietly. "Just stay in the car, okay?"

Sherise did as she was told. She watched Carlos jog up the overgrown walkway. He knocked on the door and then let himself into the raggedy, old house.

When Carlos walked in, Sherise saw a man sitting at a shoddy, old card table. The grungy man was smoking a cigarette. Or maybe a joint.

Inside the house, the man asked, “She comin’ in?” nodding toward Sherise in the car.

Carlos shook his head no. The man stood up and walked to window. He looked out. “Pretty decent car she’s in. She a good girl? You seein’ her?”

Carlos put his hands in his pockets. “Nah, she’s too good for me,” he replied. It would be nice, he had to admit. But it would never happen. Carlos pushed that thought right out of his head.

“Look, I didn’t come here to shoot the breeze. Or talk about chicks,” Carlos said.

The man nodded. He walked away from the window and back to card table. He picked up an envelope and handed it to Carlos. "I know this don't make things right between me and you. But it's the best I could do on short notice."

Carlos took the envelope, folded it, and put it in his pocket. He half thanked the man with a nod. Then Carlos turned to go. When he reached the door, the man called out to him, "Hang onto that girl, Carlos. She must be sweet on you."

Meanwhile, Sherise watched the front door of the house anxiously from the car. To distract herself, she reached back and grabbed her pink bag. She pulled out her phone. She had two missed texts from Kiki. The first text said, "Everyone knows u took off with C. Sayin u a slut."

Sherise just about dropped her phone. She bit her lip and looked back to the house. She saw Carlos coming out. She hit unlock on the car doors. Then she quickly read Kiki's second text, "At YC. Tried to cover 4 u. everyone knows u r with C.."

When Carlos got in the car, he simply said, "Go." He seemed very out of sorts.

Confused by his mood, Sherise hesitated. "Did you get the ..." she began.

But Carlos interrupted her and said, "Just *go*, okay?" Sherise put the car in drive. They got back on the freeway.

A few miles down the freeway, Sherise looked over at Carlos. He was staring out the window. He was quiet and seemed like he was somewhere else. "Carlos, Everyone knows we're together," Sherise finally said.

"Who the hell cares?" Carlos replied, still looking out he window.

"It's all over the whole school that there's somethin' goin' down between us."

Carlos shifted in his seat. He faced Sherise straight on. “What *is* goin’ down, Sherise? Why the hell are you helpin’ me anyway? Am I one of your projects? Is this a pity party or somethin’?”

Sherise blinked. She tried to think quickly. “I just wanted to help you,” she replied. “You deserve ...”

Carlos laughed. “Deserve what, Sherise? Huh? A chance with *you*?”

It took Sherise a minute to speak. “Carlos, I don’t ...”

“Yeah, that’s what I thought.”

[chapter]

5

Sherise and Carlos drove back to the city in total silence. Neither of them knew what to say. Sherise's mind raced. She worried about what everyone was saying about her and Carlos. How did they find out about them skipping school together anyway? Did she care?

That wasn't the only thing on Sherise's mind. What was going on with Carlos all of a sudden? Didn't he just walk out of that nasty house with a pocket full of cash? Why was he so distant now?

Carlos's mind was racing too. He couldn't get a read on Sherise. She was a good girl. About as good as they come these days. What could she possibly see in Carlos? What was she doing? Why was she helping him out? Was she into him? How could she be?

The drive seemed to last forever for both of them. The only sound in the car was the occasional clicking of the blinkers.

At one point, Sherise made an attempt at breaking the awkward silence. "Do you have a bank?" she asked. Sherise thought she could offer to drive him there to deposit the money.

But her question only made Carlos madder. "Yeah, I got a bank, Sherise," Carlos said, insulted by her question. "The one on Stanyan Street downtown. Know that one? That good enough, in your opinion?"

"Carlos, I only asked because I thought we could go there to ..."

"We got no time," Carlos said. He motioned to the clock on the car's dash. "You gotta be home for dinner at seven."

Sherise realized Carlos was right. But why was he being so mean to her? She just didn't understand him. It hurt so much. She wanted to cry but knew she couldn't.

Once back in the city, Carlos directed Sherise to the run-down building where he lived. Angry and frustrated, he wondered if Sherise had ever even been in his part of town before.

Sherise parked the car. "You know how to get home from here?" Carlos asked. Sherise nodded. Carlos looked out the passenger window. He saw his mom coming up the sidewalk. No way did he want Sherise and his mom meeting.

"You best roll if you're gonna make it home in time," Carlos said. "I'll holler at you later."

Before Sherise could get a word in, Carlos hopped out of the car. Sherise was floored. No thank you? No nothing? Not even a little hug for sticking her neck out for him? She couldn't believe it.

When Carlos's mom saw him get out of the car, she was full of questions. "That one of those Butler twins?" she asked Carlos. "The pretty one?"

"Uh-huh," Carlos said.

"What you doin' with her?"

"Nothin'. Never you mind. Let's go inside. I got somethin' for you."

Sherise watched Carlos talking to his mom. She looked pretty ragged, pretty hard. Sherise thought she was probably about the same age as her mom. She made Sherise feel uneasy. Sherise just had to get out of there.

Sherise put the car in drive and headed home. She couldn't get over what Carlos had said in the car. Whether or not he deserved a shot with her. What did Carlos mean? Did he want her to be his girl? Then she thought, he probably only wanted to hook up with her. That's it. Her head was spinning. Of course, she had forgotten all about the texts that were buzzing on her phone.

Sherise parked her stepdad's car on the street outside their building. She headed inside. At least she was going to be on time for dinner. And she had to admit, she was glad to be back on her home turf. Everything was cool, or so she thought.

Sherise walked in the door. Her mom and Tyson were sitting at the kitchen table, waiting for her. Sherise's heart dropped. This was bad news.

"The school called," her mom began. "They said you didn't go to your last class. *And* they said that you gave them a note. From me! A fake note, Sherise?"

Sherise lowered her head.

"We know you didn't go to yearbook club either," Tyson added. "Where were you, Sherise? What were you doing in my car?"

If Sherise told them the truth about where she was and whom she was with, she would *really* be in trouble. So, in a panic, she made up a story.

"I'm sorry," she started. "I cut school to go shopping at Eastside Mall. When I got there, they didn't have the outfit in my size. So I decided to skip YC and go to Southside Mall. I just wanted somethin' cute to wear for the—"

"*Stop,* Sherise," Tyson said. "You're grounded for ... I don't even know how long yet. Go to your room."

Sherise made her way to her room. She was sad, and now she felt horrible. She opened the door. Kiki was doing her homework.

"They already knew you were skippin' when I got home," Kiki said. "The school called 'em. I didn't rat you out. Swear. We ate without you. Tyson was so mad."

Sherise flopped down on her bed. "I think going with Carlos today was a mistake," she whispered to Kiki.

"Oh, so *now* you think?" Kiki asked.

"You were right, okay? That house I drove him to, Kiki. It was a dump. I stayed in the car."

Kiki looked up from her notebook. "Did you get my texts? Everyone knows you two cut class together. Tomorrow is goin' to be hell for you at school."

Sherise put her face into her pillow. "What was I thinking, Kiki? I'm in way over my head."

"Forget bout Carlos," Kiki said. "He's a cool guy and all. But he's trouble, Reesie. Plus, you know Tyson would never let you go out with him. *Ever.*"

Kiki was right. What was Sherise doing? She had to forget Carlos. He was bad. Plain and simple.

"I will, Kiki. I'm done," Sherise said. "It's not like he cares 'bout me anyway."

Sherise went to bed without dinner. She had a terrible night's sleep. Sherise walked into the kitchen the next morning. Her mom was drinking coffee and reading the paper. Sherise approached her slowly. "I'm so sorry, Mom," she said quietly.

But LaTreece didn't look up. "You bet you're sorry. Don't you ever forge a note from me again, young lady," she said coolly. Sherise promised that she wouldn't.

"I'm sorry I lied to Tyson too."

LaTreece set the paper down and looked up at Sherise. "You and your sister can't ... you need to behave yourselves. For a lot of reasons. Tyson's career is just one of them," she said. "He feels like he's in the spotlight now, with his job and all. He can't have you girls making trouble."

Sherise felt so ashamed. "Can I still sing? At the Meet-Up?" she asked.

"Yes, but you're absolutely grounded otherwise. Understand? For one month. Period."

Sherise accepted her punishment. She then finished getting ready for school. On the bus, her stomach started to swirl. Sherise would have to face everyone. She had no idea what to expect. She'd never been the center of nasty gossip before.

The first bell rang just after Sherise walked into class. But before she even sat down, she was told to report to the office. Once there, she knew she had to meet with Mr. Crandall, the school guidance counselor.

"Now, Sherise," Mr. Crandall started, "I haven't seen you in here since you were having trouble in math. What's going on? Why in the world did you skip yesterday?"

Sherise would never tell Mr. Crandall the truth. About anything. So she told him the same lie she told her parents. Sherise skipped school to go shopping. Mr. Crandall was appalled.

"Sherise! Do you not respect your education at all? Education is a privilege you know. Not a right. You need to start treating it with more respect. Or you will never get anywhere."

Sherise nodded silently. Damn, Mr. Crandall was such a jerk. This day really couldn't get any worse. She'd already decided it was the worst day of her life.

"You're going to have to serve two hours of detention after school every day for one week. But next time, Sherise, I won't be so easy. You know the rules. Suspension. So tell me there won't be a next time."

"There won't be a next time, Mr. Crandall," Sherise said with fire in her eyes. Mr. Crandall excused her from his office.

Sherise felt like a real loser. She'd never had detention before in her life. She went into the girls' bathroom and texted her boss, Juanita. "I have detention 4 a week after school. will b 2 hours late 2day." She then texted her mom and told her the same thing.

Feeling like crap, Sherise walked back to class. She sat down next to Tia.

"Girl, where was your head?" Tia exclaimed. "You skipped school? With Carlos? Are you crazy?"

Sherise exhaled loudly. "I know, Tia. I know. I got detention too," Sherise said. "Two hours. Every day for a week. I had to tell work and everythin'. And on top of that, I'm grounded at home for a month."

Tia couldn't believe it. She was a Latina from the wrong side trying to get ahead in this world. She wasn't going to let anything stop her. She saw Sherise's actions yesterday as a desperate girl sliding downhill just to get a stupid boy.

Tia strived to always do good and be good. She would have never driven a bad boy to a dodgy hood. Tia couldn't understand why Sherise would do such a thing. But Tia was Sherise's friend. And she would be there for her. But this was a bad situation.

After school, Sherise headed to detention. When she opened the classroom door, all the usual troublemakers turned to stare at her. Everyone looked so surprised to see Sherise Butler! She felt all eyes on her. Sherise just wanted to run. But she couldn't. Then she saw Carlos. He motioned for her to come sit by him. Sherise felt like she shouldn't. But she couldn't help herself.

"You got caught too?" Sherise whispered to him.

"Not exactly," Carlos said, smiling. "I turned myself in."

Sherise sat down at the desk next to him. She wanted to be careful. Sherise didn't want to be overly friendly. She knew it was best she stay far away from Carlos. But she just couldn't resist responding to his comment.

"You turned yourself in?" she asked. "Why?"

"Didn't want you to be in here by yourself. I even got here early to save you a spot."

That was it. That's all it took. Sherise's heart was on fire again. She liked him. She couldn't help it.

[chapter]

6

Just then Mr. Crandall yelled out, "The first rule of detention is *no talking*. I want to see everyone working. Clearly, you all weren't studying when you did whatever you did to get here. I want all of you to use this time wisely."

Sherise pulled out her math book. She could feel Carlos watching her. She was so behind! She figured she'd do as Mr. Crandall said. Sherise would use the time wisely. But just as she was getting started, Carlos passed her a note.

A note! Just like grade school! Sherise was dying to open it, but she had to wait until Mr. Crandall turned his back. When he did, Sherise opened the note. "Want to chill tonight?" it said.

Sherise added, "Yes, but I'm grounded."

She refolded the note and passed it back to Carlos. He was smiling when she handed the note to him. But after he read it, he frowned. He imagined what it was like when Sherise's parents found out she had skipped school—especially her stepdad. Carlos felt bad. He wrote back, "Did you tell them you were with me?"

Sherise said no way. Carlos was relieved. "When do I get to see you again?" he wrote back. He watched carefully as Sherise read his question. He was unsure what she would say. Would she see him again? Or was Sherise done with him after getting in so much trouble?

Carlos watched the smile grow on Sherise's face as she read his question. He knew he would see her again.

Two hours later, Mr. Crandall excused everyone from detention. Feeling better, Carlos followed Sherise out of school.

"You goin' home now?" he asked.

"No, I have to work," she said.

"Where do you work?"

Sherise smiled bashfully as she dug her name tag out of her purse. She held it up for Carlos to see.

"GG's huh?" he said. "At Southside?"

Sherise nodded.

"You takin' the bus?"

Sherise nodded again. "I don't think I will be driving the car again for a long time," she added.

"I'll roll over there with you. If you don't mind," Carlos said. "I missed practice because of detention anyway."

"But Southside Mall's in the opposite direction from your place!" Sherise said.

"So? Maybe I need to pick up some ... I don't know ... somethin' at the mall. What, you think I'm goin' out of my way just to spend time with you?" he teased her.

Sherise grinned. She was falling hard for him. No doubt about it. He was amazing! She was starting to believe that maybe he didn't just want to hook up. Maybe he really liked her! They hopped on the bus and headed to Southside Mall. Together. Sherise was in heaven.

But halfway to the mall, she started to worry. Sure, Carlos was great today. But what about yesterday? Why was he so upset on the drive home last night? It was all so odd. He turned on a dime. It didn't add up. Sherise wanted to get to the bottom of it.

"Carlos, can I ask you somethin'? 'Bout yesterday?"

Carlos looked put off. But he said, "Shoot."

"On the ride home. You seemed ... I don't know ... different. Angry."

Carlos took a deep breath. He rubbed his hands together and looked out the bus window.

"I don't like takin' money from other people," he said. "That's all."

"Did he owe it to you?"

"Sort of."

"So why do you feel bad about takin' it?"

"It's a long story, Sherise," Carlos said, still staring out the window. "Let's just say that guy owed me from way back. And will. For a long time."

Sherise could feel that Carlos didn't want to talk about this at all. But she had to keep pressing him. She liked Carlos a lot, and she just had to know what she was getting into.

"Carlos, do you do drugs? Or deal?"

Carlos turned away from the window and looked her in the eye. He was surprised by her frank question.

"It's okay if you do. But I can't ... you know ... be with you if you do."

Sherise's heart was racing. Had she just tanked her chances with him again? She hoped not. Sherise hoped Carlos would give her the answer she wanted to hear. Sherise hoped it would be the truth.

"I used to," Carlos said cautiously. Sherise looked down at her hands. At least he had told her the truth.

"People don't understand," Carlos continued, looking out the window again, "just how much money you can make. It's insane, Sherise. For real. Crazy money. And it's so *easy*."

Sherise listened carefully to every word that came out of his mouth. Carlos turned to her again. This time he was very serious.

"I'm out now, Sherise. One hundred percent. Nothin'. Done. Clean. Over and out."

With those words, Sherise's heart lifted. Images of Carlos at family dinners danced in her head. She imagined her mom saying how handsome Carlos was. She could see Carlos and Kiki playing hoops together on the courts between the Northeast Towers buildings.

"You believe me, Sherise?" Carlos asked.

Of course she did. "Yes," she replied. "I believe you, Carlos."

The bus pulled up to the mall stop. Sherise stood up. So did Carlos.

"I had a great time with you today," she said happily. "Even though it was detention and a stupid bus ride."

"Maybe someday I can take you on a real—" Sherise interrupted Carlos's suggestion. She leaned over and kissed his cheek.

"I gotta go," she said. Then she hopped off the bus and floated into work. Juanita met her at the time clock. She handed Sherise her paycheck.

"What you smilin' about? You might want to take a look at it before you get too excited," Juanita said.

Sherise told Juanita all about Carlos. How wonderful he was. How they skipped school together yesterday. How Carlos turned himself in so they could sit next to each other in detention. And how handsome and tall Carlos was.

Juanita smiled. "I suppose now you're goin' to tell me that he's rich too. And that he wants to buy you one of these?"

Juanita held up one of the houndstooth handbags. Sherise smiled. "Pretty sure I'll be buyin' my own handbags for a while," she said.

Juanita nodded in a knowing way. "Ladies gotta take care of themselves these days. Can't ever count on no man to do it."

"That's for sure," Sherise said. "Speaking of, how are these bags selling?"

"We've sold a few," Juanita said. "Sold one last night in fact."

[chapter]

7

After work, Sherise hurried right home. She was already grounded. She didn't need to cause any more trouble. When she got home, she walked in nervously. She hadn't talked to Tyson yet since all hell broke loose.

"Hey, Mom. Hey, Tyson," she said awkwardly, holding her head low. LaTreece nodded to her. Her mom looked over to Tyson. He was reading a magazine and had yet to look up.

"Tyson," Sherise began. "I'm really sorry. I'm sorry I lied. My days of skipping school are over. I promise."

Tyson closed the magazine and let it rest on his lap. "Was detention really that bad? To convince you never to skip school again?"

Sherise actually thought detention was the opposite of bad. It was amazing. It was amazing because she spent it with Carlos!

"It was okay. I mostly just caught up on math homework," she lied. The truth was that she hadn't done a bit of homework in days.

"That's good," Tyson said. He picked his magazine back up. "There are some leftovers from dinner on the counter if you're hungry."

"Okay, thanks," Sherise said, smiling at her stepdad. It took a second, but he smiled back at her. Happy to be forgiven, she headed for the kitchen. Sherise sat down alone at the table with her leftovers. She was thinking more about

Carlos than eating dinner, even though she was starving.

Kiki emerged from their bedroom and joined her at the table. "How was detention?" she asked. Sherise chewed her food slowly. She was thinking about how to answer. Kiki noticed her delay.

"What?" Kiki asked. "What's goin' on with you?"

Sherise gave Kiki a glare. She then nodded toward the living room where their parents were. "Hold on a second," Sherise said quietly. She pulled the plastic wrap back over the plate of leftovers. Sherise tucked the plate in the fridge. She motioned for Kiki to join her in their bedroom.

"He doesn't deal drugs anymore!" Sherise said excitedly behind the closed door of their shared room. "He promised! He's so cool, Kiki. I think he *really* likes me!"

Kiki raised her eyebrows in disbelief. "So you're back on that, huh? He got to you. You're not *in way over your head* anymore? I'm telling you again, Carlos is nothing but trouble."

"Kiki, get this. He rode the bus all the way to the mall with me. After detention! Oh, and he turned himself in for skippin' so I wouldn't have to be in detention alone!"

Kiki shook her head. "That's really somethin', Sherise. Whatta real prize."

"Come on, Kiki," Sherise pleaded. "He's a good guy. You'll see. Why you gotta be like that?"

"How I'm gonna be is the least of your problems," Kiki said. "If I were you, I'd be more worried about Tyson."

Kiki was right. Tyson would make seeing Carlos difficult. But for tonight, Sherise didn't care. Tonight, she felt on top of the world. It was only a matter of time before her and Carlos got together. Sherise could feel it.

The next morning at school, Sherise once again found Carlos waiting for her at her locker. "I have somethin' for you," he said. He handed Sherise a *Best of Robert Johnson* CD.

Sherise was touched. Carlos really did care about her. She knew it.

"Thanks, really," she said. "This means so much ..."

Before she could finish, Carlos put his arms around her and pulled her close. It was the kind of embrace that would never happen between two people who were just friends. Sherise wanted to melt into it, but she couldn't. She was too uptight. She could feel all eyes in the hallway on her. She wanted to be Carlos's girl. She wanted everyone to know it. But not just yet.

“What’s wrong?” Carlos asked, sensing her stiffness.

“Nothin’, I just ...”

Before Sherise could finish, she saw Nishell out of the corner of her eye. Carlos noticed how distracted Sherise was by the others in the hall. It made him furious.

“Afraid of someone seein’ us together, aren’t you?” Sherise didn’t know what to say.

“Girl can’t even be with me in the damn hallway,” Carlos said, walking away. It had been so hard for him to think that Sherise could actually like him. Just when he was starting to believe it, he realized there was no way. He felt like he was being played.

The bell rang. Sherise couldn’t move. She watched as Carlos walked away from her without another word. Everything had been so perfect just moments earlier. Now everything was all wrong. Sherise was a wreck as she walked to class. Why had she hesitated? She couldn't wait for the bell to ring so she could find Carlos. Sherise would apologize and make things right.

Carlos walked into first period study hall in a fit of rage. He was late, but Ms. Feldman, the study hall teacher, pretended not to notice. She didn't like to deal with Carlos when he was in a bad mood.

Carlos sat at a table alone. He didn't know where to look or what to do. Had Sherise changed her mind after their afternoon in detention together? And what was up with the fun bus ride? Had she gone home and decided Carlos wasn't good enough for her?

Carlos put his head down on the table. He could see it all now. Sherise got home last night. She told her stepdad about him. Then he forbid Sherise to ever see

Carlos again. He should have known not to even try with a girl as good as Sherise.

In the hall after first period, Carlos heard a voice behind him. "You look a little wound up, Carlos. Maybe I can make it better?"

Carlos looked around. It was Marnyke, flirting as usual.

"What up," he said.

"Haven't seen much of you these past few days," Marnyke said. "Some sleaze stealin' up all your time?"

"Same old, same old," he said. "You know how it goes."

Marnyke looked at him skeptically. "I hear through the grapevine you made a little run the other night. Out to your old hood. How'd that go?"

Marnyke had the biggest mouth of any girl in school. The last thing Carlos wanted was Marnyke keeping an eye on his comings and goings.

“Went all right,” Carlos replied.

“I *also* hear you got yourself a new little tag-along,” Marnyke said.

Carlos remembered when they were driving home that night that Sherise said Marnyke knew they cut class together. Was that why Sherise pulled away from him in the hallway? Was she afraid of Marnyke? Carlos really couldn’t blame Sherise if she was. Marnyke could be a real handful when she wanted to be.

Deep down, he felt that the real problem with Sherise wasn’t Marnyke. It was him. He wasn’t good enough.

Suddenly, Mr. Crandall appeared in the hallway. “Marnyke, Carlos, get to your next class,” he yelled. “You don’t want to be late.”

Marnyke glared at Mr. Crandall, but then she turned toward her next class. She looked back at Carlos. “Be careful, Carlos. Sherise don’t always know what she wants. That's all I'm sayin'. Don't let yourself get hurt." Then she walked off.

Sherise tried to find Carlos in the hall between classes, but she couldn't. In fact, that was the case the whole morning. Sherise texted him ten times. No answer. Carlos was hiding from her. That was the only answer. And Sherise didn't have time to chase after him, either. She couldn't be late for class. She had enough heat.

Sherise didn't see Carlos until lunch. She was sitting at a table with some of the girls from yearbook club when he walked in. Sherise nearly jumped out of her skin the moment she saw him. She made eye contact and tried to smile at him. But Carlos turned away from her and headed the other direction.

Tia and Kiki were discussing the yearbook layout. Sherise's mind was in another place. What should she do? Wait to talk to Carlos? Or maybe she should go right over there and apologize to him in front of the whole school? To hell with everyone and everything else.

Her mind was made up. Sherise would go right up to him and say she was really sorry. Just as Sherise was about to stand up, Marnyke sat down right beside her. Marnyke stopped Sherise dead in her tracks. Now Sherise's heart was racing faster than ever. She had no idea what Marnyke would do.

"So, Sherise," Marnyke said. "How did your ride with Carlos go the other day?"

Sherise didn't answer. Tia and Kiki looked on, nervous about the whole scene.

"Did you pick up anythin' good? Anythin' I might want to try?" Marnyke continued.

Sherise picked up her fork. "I don't have a clue what you're talkin' about, Marnyke," she said.

Marnyke laughed. "Oh, come on, girl. Don't be playin' me too. You and Carlos went down the freeway. You stopped outside a real dive. Then Carlos ran inside, right? What do you think he was doin' in there? Visitin' his granny?"

Sherise pushed her fork into some noodles. Her anger was building. In part, because it occurred to Sherise that maybe Marnyke was right. Sherise hadn't seen whatever it was Carlos picked up that day. Still, she defended Carlos.

"He's done with all that. He told me so, and I believe him. Besides, what do you care? You've got Darnell. Why you messin' in my business?"

Again, Marnyke laughed. "Don't be so not in the know, Sherise. Carlos is a kingpin. A dealer. Sorry to be the one to give you the four-one-one. I just don't want to see you make a mistake. I got your back, girlfriend."

Sherise slammed her fork down on the table. Kiki and Tia were shocked by Sherise's explosion. The whole cafeteria was watching now.

"Chill out," Marnyke teased. "It's not like you're the first girl that's given that boy a ride to make a run."

Sherise stood up and left the table. She felt upset and embarrassed. Marnyke didn't really care about her and Carlos. She just liked stirring up trouble.

But she'd also known Carlos longer than Sherise had. Maybe she knew something about him that Sherise didn't. Maybe Darnell had told her something about Carlos still dealing.

Sherise wondered if Kiki was right and her feelings for Carlos had clouded her judgment. Maybe Carlos was a no-good thug, a drug dealer. She really wanted to trust Carlos, but it was scary.

[chapter]
8

Sherise left the cafeteria in a rush. She was on the verge of tears. The cafeteria was the last place a girl wanted to be when she was in that shape. She felt like a fool. She blindly headed for her locker.

Carlos followed Sherise out of the cafeteria. He had heard the whole thing go down between Sherise and Marnyke. He had heard Sherise stick up for him. Carlos had to talk to her.

But when Carlos caught up to Sherise at her locker, she wanted nothing to do with him.

"Come on, Sherise, listen to me. I heard you stick up for me in there. No one's ever ..."

"Carlos, let's get one thing straight. I am not Marnyke. Okay? I don't get to do whatever I want, whenever I want. I don't go to wild parties. I don't do every guy in school." Sherise paused to look around before she finished, "And I sure as hell don't drive druggies around to score."

Sherise opened her locker. She dug out the CD Carlos had just given her that morning. She held it out to him. "Take this back," she said. "I don't want anything from you."

"That trip had nothing to do with drugs, Sherise. Swear."

"Whose house was it, then, Carlos? Be straight with me. Now," she demanded.

Carlos had never seen Sherise so pissed off. He decided to tell her the truth.

"My old man's," he said. Sherise was speechless.

"I didn't want you to know," Carlos said. "I'm not proud of him, okay? You saw his place. I needed money and he had some. That's it. That's the only reason I went. That man never gave me a damn thing in my life. Nothing. Not ever. For whatever reason, he decided to now. So I took it."

Sherise stood there, still holding out the CD. She was trying to decide whether or not she could believe Carlos about anything.

"Are you tellin' me that the house we went to was not the same house where you used to pick up drugs? With Marnyke? And whoever else?"

Just thinking of Marnyke driving anywhere with Carlos made Sherise cringe. Carlos exhaled loudly. Then he rested his head against the locker next to Sherise's.

"It's the same house."

Sherise lowered her arm a bit. Carlos's dad was his drug connection. She couldn't believe it.

"My family," Carlos started. "You have no idea, Sherise. It's just so messed up. This is my livin' hell. It ain't pretty, trust me. I'm sorry I didn't tell you. It just is what it is."

Carlos pulled his head away from the locker. "Keep that, okay?" he said, nodding toward the CD. "Call it taxi fare."

Then Carlos walked away. Again. Sherise looked down at the CD in her hands. Lunch hour was coming to an end. The hallway was filling up. Even though Sherise knew everyone would see her, she ran down the hall.

"Carlos, wait," she said, as she stepped in front of him. "I'm sorry I pulled away from you in the hallway this morning."

She reached her hand out toward his. She didn't know how he would react. Carlos took her hand and held it in his.

"My stepdad," Sherise started, "he's a social worker. He might be able to help your mom keep her car. Then you wouldn't have to deal with your dad anymore."

"When somethin' sounds too good to be true, Sherise, it usually is."

"Carlos, I know he's helped other people with money troubles. Come to the Meet-Up tonight. I'll introduce you to him. My mom too."

Carlos was surprised by her sudden change of heart. This girl was something else. Could he be this lucky?

"You sure you're ready for that?" he asked.

Sherise smiled. "Of course," she said.

Carlos couldn't believe it. Sherise was the best-looking, nicest girl in the whole school. And she wanted to introduce him to her parents! Carlos felt on top of the world. "All right, Sherise. I'll be there," he said.

[chapter]

9

Friday evening, Sherise and Kiki got ready for the Meet-Up together. Sherise was a ball of nerves. She stood in front of the mirror in the bathroom. Sherise raised the mascara applicator up to her left eye. But her hand was shaking so bad, she had to stop.

"Good thing you're singin' tonight and not performin' brain surgery on someone," Kiki said. "Look at your hand! You're shakin' all over!"

Sherise looked up to the bathroom ceiling and exhaled. "I always get like this before I sing. I'll be fine," she said.

Kiki shook her head. "I haven't seen you this edgy since five minutes ago."

Sherise put the applicator back in the mascara tube. "I'm gonna introduce Carlos to Mom and Tyson tonight," she said.

"Say *what*? You lost your mind for sure, girl," Kiki said.

"I like him, Kiki," Sherise said. "I want Mom and Tyson to like him too. Plus, I thought maybe Tyson could help Carlos's mom. You know, help her figure out a way to keep her car."

"Good luck with that, sister," Kiki said.

At this point, Sherise had had enough of Kiki's attitude about Carlos. More than enough in fact.

"Kiki, what the hell? Why you gotta be like that? Why are you so hard on him? And me?"

"It's not like you're gonna listen to what I say," Kiki said, "but I'll tell you anyway. I heard somethin' from Nishell today. She told me that she and Marnyke saw Carlos selling drugs."

Sherise turned back to the mirror. She pulled the mascara applicator out again and began applying it. "I'm sure they did. A long time ago," Sherise said.

Kiki shook her head. "Not a long time ago, Sherise. More like last night."

Kiki's words gave Sherise a gut-wrenching feeling in her stomach. But she still stood up for Carlos.

"Kiki, Marnyke is just makin' drama as usual. You know how she is. She probably told that lie to Nishell, knowing it would get back to me and freak me out."

"I knew you wouldn't listen," Kiki said, walking out of the bathroom.

Now alone in the bathroom, Sherise stared at herself in the mirror. She wasn't going to doubt Carlos again. No matter what anyone else said.

"Girls, let's go!" Tyson yelled from the living room. Sherise took one last look in the mirror, then headed out the door with her family. They all hopped into Tyson's car and headed to the Meet-Up. They were going early, of course, because there was a lot of setting up to do.

Sitting in the back seat, Sherise couldn't help but remember her ride in that very car with Carlos just a few days before. It was time to tell her parents about him.

"Mom, Tyson, there's someone I want you to meet. He'll be at the Meet-Up tonight. His name is Carlos Howard."

"He's a drug dealer," Kiki piped up.

"Shut your face, Kiki! He is *not*. He's a really great guy, Tyson," Sherise said. "He used to have some problems, but he's really turned his life around. For real. He's one of the best ball players at South Central High."

The conversation ended there. No one said another word the rest of the drive. The twins' phones were buzzing. But they didn't even look at them.

They arrived at the community center. The twins and LaTreece helped Tyson carry in boxes of electrical cords and other equipment. Soon it was ten minutes to seven. People were starting to arrive.

Sherise was folding up some empty paper bags backstage when she got a text message from Carlos. "**Outside**," he wrote.

Sherise headed for the door to meet him. "He's here!" she squealed to Kiki as she ran by her.

Once outside, Sherise saw Carlos standing on the sidewalk. He looked hella fine. But he looked nervous too. "I feel out of place at these things," Carlos confided. Sherise told him not to worry.

"Come on," she said, wrapping her arm in his. "It will be fine. Swear!"

Proudly, Sherise entered the community center with Carlos. Her mom saw them right away and came over to them. "You must be Carlos," she said warmly. Carlos smiled back at her.

"Wow, Mrs. Nelson. I see where Sherise gets her fine looks," he said.

"Well, how charming you are Carlos," LaTreece said. "This is my husband, Tyson."

Carlos and Tyson shook hands. They were sizing each other up, Sherise could tell.

"Tyson," Sherise said, breaking the silence, "I thought maybe you could talk to Carlos later. You might know how to help him and his mom out of a jam."

"Sure, later," Tyson said. "Excuse me now, though. Lots to do to get this event going. Sherise, sweetie, could you run out to the car and grab my tie? I left it hanging over the driver's seat. Here are the keys. LaTreece, I could use a hand backstage too. See you 'round, Carlos, after the Meet-Up."

When Sherise's parents walked away, Carlos breathed a sigh of relief.

"That wasn't so bad, was it?" Sherise asked, smiling at Carlos.

"You best go get his tie," Carlos said. Carlos seemed distant. Or was Sherise imagining things? Sherise shook it off. She headed out to the car to get Tyson's tie.

On the way back from the car, Sherise saw Carlos walk out of the community center. He headed for the back of the building. He hunched his shoulders like he didn't want to be noticed.

Sherise wondered where on earth he was going. Something must be wrong. Why would he leave without telling her, and before she sang her song too? Sherise walked along the side of the building and peeked around the corner. Carlos was meeting with some shady-looking guy. She saw Carlos take something out of his pocket. He gave it to the guy, who gave him some money. Then the guy walked off down the alley.

Sherise felt sick to her stomach. She waited for Carlos to come back around the corner. Then she let him have it.

"What the *hell* was that, Carlos?" she screamed. "Wait, you don't have to tell me because I know what I saw. You sold that guy drugs, didn't you? *Didn't you?* After I trusted you and stood up for you over and over again. I can't believe I was so stupid! Well, I'm done with you, Carlos. *Done!* Do you hear me?" She leaned against the wall, sobbing.

Humiliated and ashamed, Carlos felt like his heart was breaking. Once again, he had screwed everything up. Once again, he had destroyed his future. But he had to try to get Sherise to understand. He needed her to not hate him.

"Sherise, please let me explain. I have to tell you somethin'. I never needed money for my mom's car payment. Understand? I needed it for myself. I lied because I didn't want you to know why I needed it.

"A couple of years ago I ... I stole a car. I was high as hell, and I crashed it. No one got hurt. But I've been payin' for that car, bit by bit, ever since. It's a court order, you know. A condition of my probation. And I never missed a payment. Never. But when I quit dealin', well, it got tough. That's why I had to ask my dad for that money.

"Sherise, that day with you, I didn't pick up any drugs. I picked up cash, like I said. You hear me? Just money. It was legit. But before I could make the payment, my mom ... she ... she spent it, Sherise. I told you, my family is ... that's why I had to deal again. Okay? I had to make that money back quick and that's the only way I know how. Understand?"

Sherise was hurt, mad, and confused. She could tell Carlos was really flipped out. Part of her wanted to put her arms around him and hold him tight. But she couldn't get past the fact the he lied about dealing.

"Carlos, I don't care what you did two years ago. I just care about now, and you swore to me you weren't dealin' or usin', and it was a lie. You knew how important that was to me, and you lied anyway. I can't forgive that. I just can't trust you anymore."

"I know, Sherise," Carlos said. "I'm ... I'm sorry. I gotta go. Just forget about me. Okay?"

Then Carlos ran down the street and disappeared into the night. Sherise sadly watched him go.

Sherise slowly walked back into the community center. She was in shock. In a daze, she headed to the ladies room. She tried to think about everything Carlos had said outside. She snorted. It had probably just been more of his lies. All that mattered was that he was dealing again. Some people were just trouble. Period. That was the lesson. How could she have fallen for such a liar?

"Never again," she said to herself in the mirror. "Never again will I be that stupid." She set her purse on the counter. She opened a compact of face powder. The bathroom door opened. Marnyke, Kiki, Tia, and Nishell walked in.

"Reesie," Kiki said to her twin sister. "You okay? What happened? Where's

Carlos?" Sherise started crying. She told them about Carlos and the drugs, and how they'd all been right about him, and she'd been blind and stupid.

"I'll kill that boy!" Kiki swore, and hugged Sherise. "I'm sorry it worked out this way, sis."

The other girls tried to comfort her too. Marnyke didn't even make any of her usual nasty comments.

Finally, Kiki told Sherise to pull herself together. "It's show time," she said. "Go out and nail your song now. That will show Carlos. Right, girls?"

Tia agreed. "Oh, hell yeah," she said. "Here, let's fix your face up a little."

Minutes later, Sherise was standing just off the stage with Tia and Kiki. Tyson announced her name. Sherise stepped out onto the stage. She walked right up to the microphone.

Sherise looked out at all the people waiting for her to start. Her usual stage fright wasn't there. She was so sad and heartbroken that she didn't even feel her usual nerves. The music began. Sherise sang Robert Johnson's "Hellhound on My Trail" like she'd never sang it before.

[chapter]

10

When Sherise finished singing, the crowd was spellbound. Everyone clapped loudly and whistled for more as she made her way off of the stage. As she passed Tyson, he gave her a high five. "You've never done better, Sherise. Never," he said.

"I'm goin' home," Sherise said as she passed him. "I'll take the bus."

"Okay, see you there later," Tyson said.

As Sherise walked to the exit, a decked out woman caught her eye. Sherise knew her from somewhere. But where? Then she realized. It was Carlos's mom.

She looked a lot better than she had that day when Sherise saw her on the street. Her hair was perfectly smooth, and she was sporting a trendy houndstooth pattern handbag—the same kind that Sherise had unpacked just days ago at GG's!

"Who woulda thought," Carlos's mother began, "but damn, you know how to sing the blues, young lady. You must know a thing or two 'bout hard times and heartbreak."

Sherise stared blankly at Carlos's mother in her brand-new outfit. She suddenly understood what Carlos had tried to tell her in the parking lot. Carlos's mother had taken the money that his father had given him for his court-ordered payment. She had spent it on herself. That's why Carlos had the drugs. He was trying to make the money back.

"I do now," Sherise said coldly. Then she made her way out the door.

Sherise left the community center and walked to the bus stop. On the ride home, her mind was in a dark place. Sherise was wrestling with the sad reality. Carlos was a good guy, but he had never had a chance. Not with the parents he had and the way he was brought up.

When Sherise finally got home, she set her alarm and flopped down into her bed. She was exhausted from everything that had happened. She slept like the dead until morning. She didn't even wake up when Kiki came into the room a few hours later.

The next morning, Sherise got up as soon as her alarm went off. She got ready for work. She left the apartment much earlier than necessary for her Saturday morning shift at GG's. Luckily, her parents didn't question the time when she said good-bye to them. Sherise didn't know what she would have said if they had asked her where she was going so early. She didn't want to lie to them again. But she was on a mission.

Sherise took the bus to the Northeast Community Credit Union and cashed her paycheck. She wasn't going to use the money for that houndstooth handbag anymore, like she had thought she would. Sherise had other plans now.

Before she went in, she stopped and stood on the sidewalk for a second. Did she really want to do this? After all, she worked damn hard at GG's for her money. Her parents would have a fit if they knew what she was thinking about doing. But Sherise decided she didn't care.

Once inside the bank, Sherise looked over the half dozen tellers. She picked the youngest one. Sherise got in her line.

When it was her turn, Sherise said, "I'd like to deposit this cash into my brother's account. His name is Howard. Carlos Howard."

"What's the account number?" the teller asked.

"Oh, I can't remember it," Sherise said. Then the teller asked for Carlos's social security number.

"I don't know that either," Sherise said. "Can you please just put this money in Carlos's account? I'm tryin' to help him out. I'd give him the cash, but he wouldn't accept it. You feel me?"

Sherise slid the cash across the counter. Surprised, the young teller looked at the stack of bills. She looked back at Sherise. Moved by Sherise's generosity, the teller accepted the cash.

"I don't suppose you want a receipt?"

Sherise shook her head. "No, I don't need a receipt."

"You sure? You can use it as proof of a donation to the needy. You can write it off on your taxes I think," the teller said, typing the numbers into the computer.

"Don't need it," Sherise said. "Besides, I might not want to remember I did this later."

The teller nodded. She told Sherise to have a good day. With that, Sherise left the bank and got back on the bus to the Southside Mall. Her hands were a bit shaky, but she felt good about her decision. Carlos could use a break, after all. Sherise was happy to give him one.

Sherise arrived at work about fifteen minutes early. She saw Juanita in the small office next to the shipping and receiving room. She walked inside and sat down.

"You're early for once," Juanita winked. "I thought with you being so in love and all, you would be using every free second to be with your Mr. Perfect."

Sherise tipped her head back and looked up at the white ceiling tiles of the small office. "I don't think I'll get much time with Mr. Perfect anymore," Sherise said sadly. "Turns out Carlos is pretty much the opposite of perfect."

"Your man Carlos, is his last name Howard?" Juanita asked.

"Yeah. Why?"

"Girl, you weren't lying when you said he was handsome! So tall and fine!"

"You saw him?"

"He was in here about thirty minutes ago. Said he needed a job real bad. He insisted on an interview right then and there. Acted like he never wanted anything more in this whole world than a job here."

Sherise was confused. "What? Why?"

Juanita smiled. "I'm guessing he wants to be near you."

Sherise leaned forward in her chair. "Are you gonna hire him, Juanita?"

"I'll give it some serious thought. If he works as good as he looks, it would be worth it!" Juanita teased. "Now put your name tag on, Sherise. Go punch in now before you're late. Especially if you want to earn enough for that fine handbag!"